Love Is What It Is

LESSONS FROM EVERYDAY LIFE

GEORGE J HATCHER

CasaHatcherPress

Also By George Hatcher

Mario 1: Woman in Jeopardy

Mario 2: Coming of Age

Mario 3: Risky Business

Mario 4: Free Fall

Mario 5: Afire

Mario 6: Marked

Mario 7: Aftershock

Mario 8: Captivated

Single Titles

One Wilshire

Gabi

Rico

Cats: Meow Is The Language Of Love

HER: Artistic Expressions Through AI

Elegance In White: Through Wedding Gowns

Quinceañera Fashion: Fifteen & Fabulous

Billion Dollar Rainmaker Part I

Pages of Passion Book 1: My First 19 Years

Pages of Passion Book 2: Bold Beginnings

Pages of Passion Book 3: Rising Waves

Pages of Passion Book 4: Threads Of Destiny

Coming Soon

This book can be purchased at over 40,000 bookstores and libraries, including brick-and-mortar stores, online, in print, and digitally, including Apple and Kindle. Casa Hatcher Press is a subsidiary of Pretty Face, Inc., Rancho Mirage, California 92270.

Copyright © 2025 by George Hatcher. All rights reserved. Printed in the United States of America and abroad.

No part of this book may be used in any manner except in the case of brief quotations in critical articles or reviews.

Book and cover designed by Casa Hatcher Press

Love Is What It Is: Lessons From Everyday Life by George J. Hatcher

ISBN 979-8-9989967-6-4 (Paperback)

ISBN: 979-8-9989967-7-1 (eBook)

Dedication

Molly,

In the dance of life, you are my steady partner,

and in every melody, you are my cherished harmony.

With enduring love,

George

The Awkward First Date

The Art of Ordering the Right Drink

Ordering the right drink can feel like an art form, one that requires finesse, confidence, and just the right amount of bravado. Picture this: you're at a romantic bar, the mood is perfect, and you're ready to impress. You glance at the drink menu like it's a complex piece of modern art. Suddenly, the bartender's waiting for you to make a decision, and there you are, frozen like a deer in headlights, pondering whether a "Mojito" or "Martini" will really convey your undying love better. Spoiler alert: it won't. But fear not, dear reader, for we're here to navigate this treacherous terrain together.

First things first, let's talk about the classics. A Martini may scream sophistication, but it can also whisper "I have commitment issues." You don't want to send mixed signals while ordering. If you choose a drink that requires a twenty-step preparation and the bartender to wear a top hat, what does that say about you? It might suggest you're either a hopeless romantic or someone who's just trying too hard. Instead, go for something that reflects your personality. If you're bubbly and fun, maybe a Mimosa is your spirit drink. Just make sure you don't order it at night unless you want to be the person who perpetually lives in brunch mode.

Now let's consider the trendy options. Craft cocktails are all the rage, and you want to impress your date with your knowledge of artisanal bitters and organic garnishes. But beware! Ordering something with a name like "The Smoky Pineapple Adventure" may lead to a delightful drink or a confusing concoction that tastes like a campfire. You don't want your date thinking you're adventurous if you can't even handle a drink with a hint of smoke. Stick to drinks that sound fun but won't make you feel like you're drinking a science experiment gone wrong.

And let's not forget about the non-drinkers or those who enjoy a good mocktail. In a world where love is often represented by clinking glasses filled with something bubbly, choosing a non-alcoholic option can feel like a betrayal. But ordering a fancy mocktail can also be a bold statement. It shows that you value flavor and creativity without the need for alcohol. Plus, who doesn't love a good drink that looks like it should come with a tiny umbrella? Just be prepared for the inevitable questions about your life choices. "Are you on a cleanse? Are you pregnant? Do you just really hate fun?" Just smile and say you're embracing the 'you' without the buzz.

In conclusion, remember that the drink you order is more than just a beverage; it's a reflection of who you are and how you want to be perceived. Whether you choose a classic, a trendy mix, or a mocktail, let it be a joyous expression of yourself. Approach the bar with confidence, make your selection, and enjoy the beauty of the moment. After all, love is about connection, and if you can bond over a shared taste in drinks (or a good laugh when one of you orders something utterly ridiculous), then you're already on the right path. Cheers to love, laughter, and the delightful art of ordering the right drink!

The Rollercoaster of Relationships

The Ups: Love at First Sight (or at Least First Bite)

Love at first sight is a concept as old as time itself, often portrayed in movies with sweeping music and dreamy gazes. But let's be real: love at first bite? Now that's a true romance waiting to happen. Picture this: you're at a crowded food festival, and your eyes lock onto a sumptuous, gooey slice of pizza. The cheese is melting, the pepperoni glistens, and suddenly, all those other people fade into the background. In that moment, it's just you and the pizza, and you know this is the start of a beautiful relationship.

Now, some might argue that you can't fall head over heels for a slice of pepperoni, but those people clearly haven't experienced true culinary passion. You might think it's a bit ridiculous, but let's face it—food has the magical ability to transport us to a different state of happiness. The first bite of that pizza, where the cheese stretches and the flavors explode, can evoke feelings that no rom-com ever could. It's a moment of connection that transcends mere sustenance; it's like your taste buds are singing a duet with your heart.

Of course, not every love story is as straightforward as a pizza.

Sometimes, you take a bite of something that looks promising, only to find out it's a culinary disaster. Remember that time you were convinced that sushi was going to be your soulmate, but it turned out to be a betrayal of epic proportions? One too many seaweed-wrapped surprises, and suddenly, you're questioning everything you thought you knew about love and culinary choices. But just like in actual relationships, every bite is a lesson learned, and sometimes you have to endure a few bad meals to appreciate the good ones.

The beauty of love at first bite is that it teaches us to be adventurous. You might not know what a durian is, but you're willing to try it because, hey, life's too short to stick to boring old sandwiches. Each new dish is a potential soulmate, just waiting for you to take that leap of faith. Plus, there's something hilariously romantic about sharing a plate of food with someone special, debating the merits of pineapple on pizza while trying not to let the sauce stain your shirt. It's the little moments of laughter and shared experiences that make food—and love—so unforgettable.

So, the next time you find yourself at a restaurant or food truck, remember that love can come in many forms. Whether it's a perfectly cooked steak or a soft, warm cookie, embrace the sparks that fly when you take that first bite. Love at first sight may be the stuff of dreams, but love at first bite? Now that's a flavor to savor. So go ahead, indulge in your culinary crushes, and who knows? You might just discover that the most delicious romances are found not just in the eyes, but also on your plate.

The Downs: Misunderstandings That Could Fill a Novel

In the grand romantic comedy that is life, misunderstandings often take center stage, making you wonder if love comes with a manual—or at least a comedy script. Picture this: two people are madly in love, gazing into each other's eyes at a cozy café. One partner leans in and whispers sweet nothings while the other mishears "I love your zest for life" as "I love your chest hair." Cue the awkward laughter and a sudden need for a haircut. These small yet hilarious blunders can lead to epic tales that would make even Shakespeare chuckle in his grave.

Let's not forget the classic case of the "texting misfire." You know the drill: your partner sends a message intended for you, but instead, it lands in the chat with your mother. "Can't wait to see you tonight, baby! I'll wear that outfit you like." Suddenly, your mom is left questioning your fashion choices and deciding whether it's too late to schedule a therapy session. And just when you thought your relationship was filled with romance, it turns into a family sitcom where everyone's in on the joke—except for your mom, who is now convinced you've joined a secret nudist colony.

Then there's the notorious "I thought you meant..." scenario. You ask your partner what they want for dinner, and they respond with "surprise me." You take this as an invitation to whip up your famous burnt lasagna, only to find them horrified and questioning your culinary skills. "Surprise" in this case was not the thrill of an unexpected meal but rather the horror of a kitchen disaster. The laughter that ensues might just be the glue that keeps your relationship strong—or at least the reason you both decide to order takeout next time.

Don't even get me started on the misunderstandings that arise from watching romantic films together. One partner might get swept up in the emotional whirlwind of a tear-jerker, while the other is just trying to figure out why the protagonist hasn't yet realized that love is not about grand gestures but rather about who takes out the trash. The tears flow, the popcorn flies, and by the end of the movie, you're left with a heartwarming moment where you both realize that love is about compromise—like agreeing to watch an action flick next time to avoid any more emotional rollercoasters.

In the end, these misunderstandings are the quirks of love that make relationships uniquely entertaining. They're the stories you'll share at gatherings, the moments that become your inside jokes, and the experiences that remind you that love isn't just about perfect harmony. It's about the delightful chaos that comes with two imperfect people trying to navigate life together. So, embrace the misfires, the awkward moments, and the ridiculous misunderstandings—they're all part of the beautiful mess that is love.

The Loop-de-Loops: Surviving the Crazy Ex Stories

Ah, the crazy ex stories—those rollercoaster rides that can leave you dizzy and questioning your life choices. You know, the ones that make you feel like you've just stepped off a spinning ride at the county fair, clutching your stomach and wondering how you ended up here. Everyone has at least one story that could make a great movie plot, complete with unexpected twists, dramatic music, and maybe even a talking animal for comic relief. Surviving these tales of love gone wrong is not just a rite of passage; it's practically an Olympic sport.

First up, let's talk about the ex who took "keeping in touch" to a whole new level. You know the type—one minute you're enjoying a quiet evening with a pint of ice cream, and the next, your phone lights up with a "just checking in" text at 2 a.m. This ex has a PhD in passive-aggressive messages and a black belt in "I'll be there in five minutes" surprises. You might find yourself wondering if they've secretly enrolled in a course called "How to Make Your Ex's Life a Living Hell." The best strategy here? Perfect the art of the polite but firm "I'm busy" response, while mentally drafting your future memoir titled "The Night My Ex Tried to Burn Down My New Relationship."

Then there's the ex who seems to have a sixth sense for when you're finally moving on. Just when you've perfected your new dating profile and are ready to dive back into the dating pool, this ex swoops in like a superhero with a cringe-worthy backstory. They'll send you a message that's either a nostalgic trip down memory lane or a desperate plea to rekindle the flame, complete with a montage of your best moments together. You're left wondering if they've been lurking in the shadows like a romantic ninja, just waiting for their moment to strike. Remember, folks, it's all about timing. Your best defense is a good offense: a witty come-back that will leave them reeling and questioning their life choices.

Now, let's discuss the ex who has an uncanny ability to find love in the most unexpected places. You're scrolling through social media, minding your own business, when you stumble upon their engagement announcement. You do a double take, squint at the screen, and then spill your drink all over your keyboard. How did they go from "we're just not meant to be" to planning a wedding with someone who looks like they belong in a magazine? It's almost as if they've been secretly collecting relationship points while you were busy healing your heart. The key here is to embrace the absurdity. Send them a congratulatory message that's dripping with sarcasm and a hint of genuine happiness—because the universe has a funny way of balancing things out.

Finally, we can't forget about the ex who refuses to let go of the past. They pop up at the most inconvenient moments, like a bad sequel to a movie that should have ended after the first installment. Whether it's at a mutual friend's wedding or your favorite coffee shop, they'll always find a way to remind you of the time they "accidentally" set your favorite sweater on fire. Surviving these encounters requires a solid game plan: practice your best "I'm doing great" smile while internally chanting, "This too shall pass." Remember, love is a loop-de-loop, and sometimes you just have to hold on tight and enjoy the ride, even if it makes your stomach churn.

So, here's the takeaway: surviving the crazy ex stories is all about perspective, humor, and a little bit of resilience. These experiences, while often cringe-worthy, are part of the colorful tapestry of love that makes life so entertaining. Embrace the chaos, share your own tales, and above all, keep your sense of humor intact. After all, love is what it is, and sometimes, it's a wild, winding ride filled with unexpected surprises that make the journey all the more memorable.

Love Languages: The Dialects of Affection

Words of Affirmation: Sweet Nothings and Awkward Compliments

Words of affirmation can sometimes feel like a linguistic dance, a delightful waltz where the right words can sweep someone off their feet, and the wrong ones can trip them up like a clumsy giraffe on roller skates. We've all been there, trying to muster up the courage to say something sweet, only to have it tumble out awkwardly, like a cat attempting to fit into a too-small box. "You have the most beautiful smile" is great, but when it comes out as "Your teeth are really... white!" it can lead to a moment of silence that's only broken by the sound of crickets chirping.

Let's not forget the classic "sweet nothings." These are the saccharine phrases that can melt hearts faster than ice cream on a summer day. However, we must tread carefully because not all sweet nothings are created equal. Telling someone, "You make my heart race like a hamster on a wheel" might elicit giggles rather than swoons. It's all about context. The ideal sweet nothing should be like the perfect slice of cake: just the right amount of sweetness, with a sprinkle of charm, and definitely not something that makes you question the baker's sanity.

Then there are awkward compliments, which are like the surprise twist at the end of a rom-com—unexpected and sometimes cringeworthy. Picture this: you're at a party, and you spot someone looking particularly dapper. Instead of a simple "You look nice," you blurt out, "That shirt is so bright it could guide ships to shore!" While you might think you're being clever, the recipient could be left wondering if they should thank you or seek out a lighthouse for assistance. Awkward compliments can turn a potentially romantic moment into a scene straight out of a sitcom.

Finding the right balance between genuine affection and humorous awkwardness can be a challenge. The key lies in knowing your audience. If your partner appreciates a good dad joke or enjoys the occasional pun, you might hit the sweet spot with, "You're the peanut butter to my jelly—without you, I'm just a boring piece of bread!" However, if your partner is more of a romantic poet, they might roll their eyes at your sandwich analogy and wish you'd stuck to something more heartfelt. It's a fine line between endearing and bewildering, like a cat trying to hug a dog.

In the end, words of affirmation are a powerful tool in the love toolkit. They can build someone up or leave them wondering if they accidentally wandered into a comedy club instead of a romantic rendezvous. So, the next time you feel the urge to shower your beloved with sweet nothings or compliments, remember to keep it light and playful. After all, laughter is one of love's greatest companions—just make sure your jokes don't leave them searching for the nearest exit!

Acts of Service: The Dishes that Spell Romance

In the grand symphony of romance, there's an unsung hero that often goes unnoticed: the humble act of doing the dishes. Yes, you heard that right! While most people think romance is all about candlelit dinners and moonlit walks, nothing says "I love you" quite like a sparkling clean kitchen. Picture this: your partner walks in, and there you are, suds flying, singing off-key, and doing a little dance while scrubbing the pots. It's like a romantic comedy, but with less chance of winning an Oscar and more likelihood of winning a heart.

Now, you might be wondering why dishes are the secret ingredient to a successful romantic recipe. Well, let's break it down. When you take the time to wash away the remnants of last night's lasagna, you're not just cleaning; you're demonstrating love in action. It's the equivalent of writing a sonnet, except instead of paper and ink, you've got sponges and dish soap. And let's be honest, nothing says "I'm in this for the long haul" like tackling the crusty remains of dinner together. Just imagine the bonding moments as you argue over whether to soak or scrub. That's the stuff love stories are made of!

Of course, the real magic happens when you surprise your partner by tackling the dishes without being asked. It's like finding out that the pizza delivery guy also moonlights as a magician because, poof, the dishes are done and the kitchen sparkles! Your partner will look at you with a mix of disbelief and adoration, as if you've just pulled a rabbit out of a hat. "Who knew you had it in you?" they might say, and you can reply with a wry smile, "I've been practicing for this moment my entire life."

Now, let's not forget the charming debates that arise from dish duty. Who knew that a simple chore could lead to such passionate discussions? "I believe plates should be stacked this way!" versus "No, clearly it's this way!" It's as if you're reenacting a scene from a courtroom drama, complete with exaggerated gestures and a flair for the dramatic. And while you might be tempted to turn it into a full-blown argument, just remember: the goal is to clean the dishes, not to win a Pulitzer Prize for the best debate performance.

In the end, acts of service like doing the dishes are more than just chores; they're opportunities for connection and laughter. So, the next time you find yourself staring down a mountain of dirty dishes, remember that you're not just cleaning; you're crafting a romantic masterpiece. And who knows? You might even find that the best moments in your relationship are forged not in grand gestures but in those everyday acts that spell love—like washing away the remnants of dinner together, one soapy dish at a time.

Gifts: When a Coffee Mug Means "I Love You"

In the grand tapestry of romance, few gifts say "I love you" quite like a coffee mug. Sure, diamonds are forever, but have you ever tried sipping your morning brew from a diamond-encrusted mug? Spoiler alert: it's not as practical as it sounds, and you might end up with more than just a caffeine buzz. A coffee mug, on the other hand, is a daily reminder of affection. It's a vessel for warmth, comfort, and the occasional accidental spill that leads to a sweeping declaration of "I love you" from the floor when you realize your favorite mug is now an abstract art piece.

Choosing the right coffee mug can feel like a relationship itself. You start by browsing through endless options online, trying to find one that encapsulates your partner's essence. You might come across a mug that says "World's Okayest Partner" and think, "Perfect!" But then, you remember that love is not just about settling for okay. You want a mug that sparks joy, one that elicits a grin every morning, even if it's just because it features a cat wearing a sombrero. Remember, laughter is the best seasoning for love, and what better way to spice up breakfast than with a quirky mug?

The real beauty of gifting a coffee mug is in the little things. It's not just a present; it's an opportunity for connection. Picture this: you hand your beloved the mug, and they take a moment to read the silly slogan written on it. They chuckle, and in that moment, you've created a shared memory, a bond over the ridiculousness of life. Each time they sip coffee from that mug, they're not just getting their caffeine fix; they're reminded of your thoughtful gesture and the laughter it brought. It's like a daily love note that says, "Hey, remember that time you almost choked on your coffee because of my terrible joke? Good times!"

Of course, there are risks involved in gifting a coffee mug. For instance, you might accidentally choose one with a message like "I'm Not a Regular Mom, I'm a Cool Mom," which can lead to a series of eye rolls and an immediate conversation about how you should probably just stick to standard gifts like socks. But isn't that part of the fun? Love is about navigating those awkward moments together, and if your partner can laugh at the mug you so enthusiastically gifted, then they're probably a keeper. After all, what's love without a little bit of humor and the occasional cringe?

In the end, a coffee mug is more than just ceramic; it's a symbol of love, laughter, and the everyday moments that make life beautiful. So the next time you're pondering what to get your significant other, remember that a simple mug can hold more than just coffee. It can hold memories, laughter, and perhaps even a few secrets shared over steaming cups of joe. Love is what it is, and sometimes it's as simple as a warm beverage and a silly mug that says, "You're the cream in my coffee."

Communication: The Love Signal

Texting: The New Love Letter

Texting has become the modern-day equivalent of the love letter, minus the wax seal and romantic candlelight. Gone are the days when you would spend hours crafting the perfect note, only to have it delivered by a friend who might drop it in the mud on the way to your crush. Now, with just a thumb, you can hit send and have your heartfelt (or hastily written) sentiments delivered in an instant. Sure, the romance of handwritten prose may have its charm, but let's be honest: nothing says "I love you" quite like a perfectly timed GIF of a cat falling off a table.

The beauty of texting is that it caters to our desire for immediacy. We no longer need to wait for the mailman to deliver our feelings; instead, we can share our innermost thoughts while standing in line at the grocery store. What's more romantic than typing "I miss you" while debating whether to buy organic or regular bananas? And let's not forget the thrill of receiving a text from that special someone. That little vibration in your pocket feels like a mini rollercoaster ride of emotions. You open it, heart racing, only to find they've sent you a meme about how they love pizza more than people. Ah, true love.

Yet, texting can also be a minefield of miscommunication. A simple "K" can send your heart plummeting into a chasm of despair. Did they mean "Okay, cool" or "Okay, I'm done with this conversation"? The ambiguity of text can turn even the most confident lover into a detective, analyzing every punctuation mark like it holds the secrets of the universe. "Why didn't they add an exclamation point? Are they mad at me? Should I send a follow-up emoji?" The possibilities are endless, and let's be real, it's enough to drive anyone a little bonkers.

And let's not overlook the art of the emoji. Those little yellow faces have transformed how we express love and affection, but they come with their own set of challenges. Do you go for the classic heart, or is that too cliché? Maybe a winking face will convey your playful nature? But heaven forbid you accidentally send a peach emoji instead of a heart, and suddenly your sweet nothings take a very different turn. Love in the age of texting requires a PhD in emoji linguistics, and even then, you might just end up in the awkward zone of misunderstanding.

In the end, texting may not replace the timeless charm of a love letter, but it certainly adds a layer of hilarity to modern romance. Whether it's misinterpreted messages or the thrill of a new notification, the digital love letter is here to stay. So embrace the chaos, laugh at the misunderstandings, and remember that love, in all its forms, is still what it is—a beautiful, messy, and often hilarious journey.

The Power of Emojis: Heart Eyes and Facepalms

In the grand theater of modern romance, emojis have taken center stage, wielding the power to convey emotions faster than you can say "I love you." Picture this: you're on a first date, and as your date tells a charming story about their cat, you send a heart eyes emoji. Suddenly, they think you're ready to adopt a feline family together! But fear not, for emoji miscommunication is the spice of dating. That heart eyes icon can express admiration, or it could just mean you're really into their dessert choice. It's a fine line between affection and dessert envy!

Now, let's talk about the infamous facepalm emoji. This little gem has the power to encapsulate our most cringeworthy moments in love. Whether it's accidentally texting your crush a meme meant for your best friend or confusing their name with your ex's, a well-placed facepalm can say "Oops, I did it again" without the need for a full-blown apology. It's a universal signal that says, "I'm human, I mess up, but here's a light-hearted way to acknowledge it." In a world where we all want to appear polished, the facepalm is a refreshing reminder that we're all just a little bit ridiculous.

Then there's the joy of using emojis to spice up those mundane love notes. Sending a simple "Thinking of you" can easily be transformed into an epic love declaration with the right combination of emojis. A heart, a slice of pizza, and a dancing cat can convey that you think of your partner as the ideal companion for both romance and late-night snacks. Who wouldn't want to be the subject of such culinary affection? Suddenly, love notes become a cryptic puzzle that requires a decoder ring. "What does the taco mean?" you might ask, only to realize it symbolizes your taco Tuesday tradition. Nothing says love like food!

Of course, emojis can also help you navigate the treacherous waters of dating. Imagine receiving a text that reads, "I had a great time last night 😊" versus "I had a great time last night." The former gives you butterflies and makes you feel like you're starring in a rom-com, while the latter feels like a polite nod from an acquaintance. The right emoji can transform a simple message into a heartfelt declaration, turning an everyday conversation into a page from a love story. It's like giving your words a makeover, complete with a sparkling new outfit and a dash of charisma!

Finally, we must acknowledge that with great power comes great responsibility. With the emoji palette at our fingertips, it's easy to misfire. So before you send that wink emoji to your significant other, pause for a moment and think, "Am I trying to flirt or just acknowledging how cute their new haircut is?" The line between romantic interest and friendly banter can be as thin as a strand of spaghetti. In the end, emojis are the delightful, chaotic, and sometimes confusing symbols of love in the digital age. Embrace the heart eyes and facepalms, for they are the laughter and joy woven into the tapestry of our romantic adventures!

The Joy of Miscommunication: When "What's for Dinner?" Becomes a Debate

In relationships, the simple question "What's for dinner?" can quickly escalate into a full-blown debate worthy of the most heated political forums. It starts innocently enough, with one partner innocently looking for a meal to satisfy their hunger. But as soon as the words leave their lips, it's as if they've thrown a match onto a pile of dry leaves. Suddenly, dinner is no longer just a meal; it becomes a battleground of preferences, dietary restrictions, and culinary aspirations. The room fills with the tension of unspoken expectations and the faint sound of a clock ticking down to an inevitable showdown.

The first miscommunication often arises from the sheer vagueness of the question itself. One partner might be thinking of a gourmet three-course meal, while the other is dreaming of a quick bowl of cereal. It's like asking a toddler what they want to do today —good luck getting a straight answer! You may end up with a request for "something delicious" that could range from sushi to a peanut butter sandwich. As each partner tries to navigate the minefield of choices, simple dinner plans morph into a whimsical guessing game. It's a comedy of errors where one person's "spaghetti" is another's "vegan gluten-free noodle surprise," leading to confusion and, of course, laughter.

Then comes the inevitable blame game. If one partner suggests tacos and the other admits to hating them, you can hear the collective sigh of disappointment echoing through the house. "How could you not like tacos?" becomes a rhetorical question loaded with the weight of unmet expectations. Suddenly, dinner has morphed into a reflection of personal values and past traumas—because let's face it, who knew that a simple meal could unveil the intricacies of one's childhood experiences with food? The joy of miscommunication shines through as couples realize they're not just negotiating a meal; they're navigating a complex web of emotions and preferences that they never even knew existed.

As the clock ticks closer to dinner time, the stakes get higher. Each suggestion feels like a risk, and soon both partners find themselves in a culinary stand-off reminiscent of a classic Western stand-off. "I could make a mean stir-fry," one might suggest, while the other rolls their eyes as if the very idea is an affront to their palate. At this point, it's less about dinner and more about pride. The laughter bubbles up as they realize they're debating like politicians, except the stakes involve not only their dinner plans but also the prospect of an evening filled with takeout menus and fridge raids.

Ultimately, the joy of miscommunication in the realm of meal planning serves as a reminder that love is not just about romance and shared dreams. It's also about the humorous, sometimes absurd moments that arise from the everyday. Every debate over dinner is a chance to learn about each other, to embrace quirks, and to laugh at the chaos of life together. In the end, whether it's tacos, stir-fry, or cereal, it doesn't matter as long as there's love, laughter, and perhaps a little takeout on the table. After all, isn't that what love is all about?

The Family Factor

Meeting the Parents: A Comedy of Errors

Meeting the parents can feel like stepping onto a stage where the stakes are high, and the script is entirely improvised. As the day approached, I couldn't help but imagine my partner's family as a quirky sitcom cast, complete with oddball characters and laugh tracks. I envisioned the father as a gruff but lovable figure, the mother as the ultimate homemaker, and maybe even a sibling who would keep throwing in snarky one-liners. I felt like I was preparing for an audition, and I was determined to steal the show. Little did I know, I was about to become the comic relief.

The day finally arrived, and I rolled up to their house with a bouquet of flowers that looked like they had been through a windstorm. I confidently knocked on the door, only for it to swing open to reveal my partner's younger sibling, who was dressed like they had just walked out of a video game. After a moment of silence, they burst into laughter, pointing at my wilted bouquet. I tried to play it cool, claiming it was an avant-garde statement on the fleeting nature of love, but I could feel my face heating up like a toaster. The sibling's chuckles echoed in my ears as I stepped inside, already regretting my choice of gift.

As I settled into the living room, I quickly realized that the family dynamic was like an elaborate game of charades. My partner's father cracked jokes that flew over my head, while the mother seamlessly transitioned from discussing her favorite hobbies to asking me about my life goals, all without a breath in between. I felt like I was undergoing a verbal obstacle course, dodging questions and trying to keep my cool as I spilled my half-baked ideas about starting a podcast. Who knew that discussing my love for obscure 80s bands could lead to such an intense interrogation about my future?

The pinnacle of my comedic misadventures came when dinner was served. The table was beautifully set, and I was both in awe and terrified. As I reached for what I thought was a bread roll, I accidentally sent a bowl of mashed potatoes flying across the room. Time seemed to slow down as I watched the creamy mass splatter against the wall, creating what could only be described as a modern art masterpiece. The room erupted in laughter, and instead of feeling mortified, I joined in. After all, who couldn't appreciate a little culinary chaos? If anything, I was now part of the family story, the "potato incident" that would be retold at gatherings for years to come.

By the end of the evening, I had survived the gauntlet of parental scrutiny and emerged with a newfound appreciation for the unpredictability of love. Meeting the parents was less about impressing them with my charm and more about embracing the hilarity of the situation. As I left, I could hear the family still chuckling about my mashed potato disaster. It was a reminder that love isn't just about the perfect moments; it's also about the perfectly imperfect ones. And just like that, I realized that in the grand comedy of love, sometimes the best scenes are the ones that go completely off-script.

Family Gatherings: Love or Hostage Situation?

Family gatherings: the events that promise laughter, food, and a healthy dose of chaos. It's a delightful paradox where love meets the reality of long-lost relatives asking if you've found a job yet or when you'll finally settle down. The air is thick with the smell of Grandma's famous casserole, and the tension might be just as palpable as the aroma. You can practically hear the collective sighs of family members as they brace themselves for the inevitable questions that feel more like an inquisition than a casual chat. Love may be in the air, but so is the smell of Aunt Edna's tuna salad that no one asked for.

Picture this: you walk into a room filled with family members who haven't seen you since the last holiday gathering, and suddenly, you're the star of a reality show called "Guess What You're Doing Wrong with Your Life." Cousins who once played tag in the backyard now seem to have PhDs in unsolicited advice. The pressure to explain your life choices can turn a simple "How have you been?" into a multi-act play of justifications. Who knew that loving your job as a barista could evoke such deep concern? "But honey, you can't live on coffee alone!" they say, oblivious to the fact that you do, indeed, survive on coffee and dreams.

Then there's the charming tradition of family games. Nothing says "we love each other" quite like a heated game of charades where Uncle Bob insists on using interpretive dance to convey "The Godfather." Watching him flail around while everyone else tries to guess is a comedy goldmine, but it's also a reminder of how family gatherings can morph into a competitive sport. The stakes are high, and suddenly you're rooting for your team while trying to avoid the awkward eye contact with Grandma, who is convinced that your team has a distinct advantage—mostly because you're younger and, in her eyes, inherently more clever.

Let's not forget the heartwarming yet utterly exhausting tradition of group photos. The moment the camera clicks, you can almost hear the collective groan as everyone attempts to strike a pose that says, "We're the perfect family" while simultaneously thinking, "Please don't post this on social media." The kids are crying, the dog has run off with the neighbor's sandwich, and someone's wearing a sweater that could only be described as a crime against fashion. Yet, in the midst of this chaotic scene, you can't help but feel a warm glow of affection. You're all in this together, facing the absurdity of life with a shared bond that somehow makes it all worthwhile.

In the end, family gatherings are a delightful mix of love and hostage situation vibes. You might leave with a headache from the noise and an eye twitch from the questions, but you'll also carry with you the laughter, the memories, and maybe even a few leftover slices of pie. Love is indeed what it is—messy, hilarious, and often overwhelming—but it's those very moments that remind us of what family is all about. So, the next time you find yourself at a family gathering, embrace the chaos. After all, it's all part of the beautiful, bizarre tapestry of love that binds us together.

Sibling Rivalry: Can Love Really Conquer All?

Sibling rivalry is like the ultimate reality show that runs in every household, complete with plot twists, dramatic confrontations, and surprise alliances. You've got your classic scenarios: the battle for the last piece of pizza, the eternal debate over who gets the biggest slice of cake, or the well-timed snatch of a toy just as the other sibling is about to reach for it. It's a competition that never truly ends, even when the siblings grow up and are supposed to be "mature." Spoiler alert: maturity is overrated, especially when there's a chance to throw shade at your brother's questionable haircut from 1995.

As the years roll on, these sibling rivalries transform into a sort of comedic routine. You've got your two main characters—the overachiever and the underachiever. The overachiever is usually the one who can do no wrong, with a resume that reads like a super-hero's biography, while the underachiever is perfecting the art of procrastination, often with a bag of chips in one hand and the TV remote in the other. Yet, amid this chaotic comedy, there's a question that looms large: can love really conquer all, or is it just a clever tagline for a rom-com?

The truth is, love gets put to the test more often than an awkward family gathering. Picture this: the overachiever finally invites the underachiever to a fancy dinner party, and the underachiever shows up in sweatpants, ready to raid the snack table. Cue the eye rolls and the whispered critiques. But deep down, there's an unspoken bond that often shines through the chaos. Love is that invisible force that somehow allows the overachiever to look past the sweatpants and the chips and still hope for a decent conversation. It's the subtle acknowledgment that, no matter how many competitive jabs are thrown, they are still family.

Sibling rivalry can sometimes morph into that unique blend of love and annoyance, where the love is always there but often buried under layers of teasing and playful insults. It's the kind of love that can survive a thousand eye rolls and a million sarcastic comments. The bond is fortified through shared childhood memories of teaming up against the parents, and those ridiculous inside jokes that no one else gets. In many ways, it's like a rollercoaster ride—thrilling and nauseating all at once, but absolutely unforgettable.

In the end, the question remains: can love indeed conquer all? Well, if love can survive the countless battles over who gets to sit in the front seat during family road trips, or who can claim the TV remote during family movie night, then yes, love can conquer sibling rivalry. It may not mean that the rivalry will ever completely vanish, but love will ensure that there's always a safety net ready to catch the falling comedies of life, proving that even in the most intense sibling rivalries, love is what it is—messy, chaotic, but oh-so-necessary.

The Friends' Influence

The Wingman: Your Best Friend or Your Worst Enemy?

The wingman: a title that carries more weight than the average person might realize. One minute, they're helping you score that dreamy date at the bar; the next, you're left wondering if they're secretly trying to sabotage your love life for their own amusement. Let's face it, the role of the wingman can be as slippery as a banana peel on a dance floor. You think they've got your back, but there's always that chance they'll trip you up instead, just for kicks.

Picture this: you're at a party, heart racing, and you spot the perfect potential partner across the room. You summon your courage and prepare to make your move. Enter the wingman, who's supposed to swoop in with suave confidence and distract the competition. Instead, they start an impromptu karaoke session, belting out off-key 80s hits, drawing all attention away from you. You're standing there, contemplating if it's possible to disappear into thin air while your wingman is living their best life, completely oblivious to your internal crisis.

Now, let's not forget the infamous "helpful advice" that wingmen love to dispense. Just when you think you're about to impress someone with your dazzling wit, your wingman jumps in with their own version of charm. "Oh, you like hiking? My friend here has climbed Mount Everest—twice!" Suddenly, you're in a competition you didn't sign up for, and your wingman is playing the role of the overzealous hype man. You're left wondering if they're really trying to help or if they just enjoy watching you sweat.

Of course, not all wingman experiences are disastrous. Sometimes, they're the unsung heroes of your love life, swooping in with the perfect icebreaker or a hilarious anecdote that makes you look like a total catch. They can help you navigate the treacherous waters of awkward small talk and even give you that much-needed pep talk when you're feeling like a romantic disaster. A good wingman knows when to step back and let you shine, like a supportive sidekick in a rom-com, but only if they don't get too carried away with their own antics first.

In the end, the true test of a wingman lies in their ability to make you laugh at the absurdity of it all. Whether they're your best friend or your worst enemy, having someone by your side during the wild ride of dating can turn a potential disaster into a memorable adventure. So, the next time you're gearing up for a night out with your wingman, remember to brace yourself for anything and everything. After all, love is what it is, and sometimes it's a comedy of errors with a side of friendship.

Friends vs. Lovers: The Ultimate Showdown

When it comes to the age-old debate of friends versus lovers, it's a bit like comparing apples and oranges—if those apples were occasionally bruised and the oranges could sometimes throw a tantrum. Friends are the ones who help you move your couch, while lovers are the ones who help you move on after that couch-related existential crisis. Friends provide the comfort of knowing that your secrets are safe, while lovers? Well, they might just turn those secrets into the plot of a romantic comedy that no one asked for.

Imagine a friend who knows you so well that they can finish your sentences. This is great until you realize they also know that your favorite late-night snack is a questionable combination of pickles and peanut butter. Enter the lover, who is charming enough to not judge your midnight cravings but just intrusive enough to suggest you try something fancier, like avocado toast—because clearly, they want to change the world one meal at a time. The friends are there for the "I can't believe they said that!" moments, while lovers are there for the "I can't believe I said that!" moments, creating a delightful cocktail of shared embarrassment.

But what happens when your best friend starts to look a little too much like a romantic interest? Suddenly, the comfortable banter transforms into a high-stakes game of emotional dodgeball. You're dodging the terrifying thought of ruining the friendship while also trying to catch those butterflies that seem to have taken up residence in your stomach. Spoiler alert: this is where the real confusion begins. Friends are safe harbors in the stormy seas of love, but lovers? They're the wild waves that might just sweep you off your feet—if you can survive the riptide of awkwardness first.

Let's not forget the classic "friend zone" dilemma. It's a place so notorious that it deserves its own zip code. Friends may offer you sage advice on how to navigate your feelings, but they also know that if you ever used the term "friend zone" in their presence, they might just roll their eyes so hard they see their brain. Lovers, however, are often the ones who capitalize on that awkwardness, throwing around phrases like "we need to talk" as if they're auditioning for a soap opera. The dramatic tension can be palpable, leading to moments that make you wonder if you should have just stuck to Netflix and ice cream with your friends.

In the end, friends and lovers have their own unique charm, like chocolate and vanilla ice cream. You may love one flavor, but sometimes a scoop of both is necessary to satisfy your cravings. Friends offer a safety net, while lovers throw you into the circus of romance, complete with clowns and cotton candy. So, whether you find yourself laughing with friends or swooning with lovers, just remember that love, in all its forms, continues to be the ultimate showdown—one that brings both laughter and a few bumps and bruises along the way.

Advice from Friends: The Good, the Bad, and the Hilarious

When it comes to love, friends can be the most entertaining and, at times, bewildering source of advice. They come armed with their own experiences, which can range from the absolutely brilliant to the downright absurd. Picture this: your best buddy, fresh off a breakup, proclaims that the key to moving on is to "date someone who looks like your ex but is definitely taller and has a dog." While the logic may be questionable, you can't help but chuckle at the absurdity of it all. Friends have a unique way of turning heartbreak into a comedy show, making you laugh even when you feel like crying.

Then there are those moments when the advice transcends ridiculousness and veers straight into the realm of the downright unhelpful. Your well-meaning friend who's never been in a serious relationship might suggest that all you need is to "just relax and be yourself." Sure, because nothing says romance quite like showing up on a date wearing pajamas and discussing your favorite Netflix series. It's these gems of wisdom that remind us that sometimes, it's best to take advice with a grain of salt—or perhaps an entire salt shaker—especially when it comes from someone whose idea of commitment is keeping a houseplant alive for more than a week.

Of course, not all advice is created equal, and there are those rare moments when your friends hit the nail on the head. These nuggets of wisdom often come wrapped in humor, like when your friend says, "If you want to keep the spark alive, just remember to never stop flirting. Even if it's just with the pizza delivery guy." This kind of playful banter serves as a reminder that love should be fun and lighthearted. It's the kind of advice that makes you realize that in the grand scheme of things, laughter can be just as important as romance itself.

Let's not forget the circus of group chats where love advice flows like a bottomless cup of coffee. One minute, you're discussing your feelings, and the next, your friends are sending memes that perfectly capture the chaos of dating. "When you finally meet the one, but they have bad taste in music" paired with a GIF of someone dramatically fainting is the kind of relatable humor that makes love seem a little less daunting. These moments highlight that while love can be complicated, it's also filled with shared experiences that are often best laughed at together.

In the end, the beauty of seeking advice from friends lies in the blend of the good, the bad, and the hilariously absurd. Each piece of advice, no matter how ridiculous, adds to the tapestry of your love life. So the next time you find yourself in a sticky romantic situation, remember to call up your friends, share a laugh, and embrace the chaos. After all, love is what it is, and sometimes, it's best approached with a hearty dose of humor and a willingness to take things less seriously.

The Mundane Moments

Grocery Shopping: The Ultimate Love Test

Grocery shopping is often considered a mundane chore, but let's be honest—it's the ultimate love test. Forget about candlelit dinners and romantic getaways; the real measure of your relationship can be found in the dairy aisle. Picture this: you and your partner stroll into the store, hand in hand, ready to tackle the week's meals. But just a few moments later, you're both staring at a wall of cereal boxes like you're deciphering hieroglyphics. This is where the love begins to show cracks or, if you're lucky, flourishes like a well-watered houseplant.

As you navigate through the aisles, the first test of love emerges: the cart. Is it a two-person operation, or does one person take over while the other pretends to read the ingredients on the back of a snack? If your partner starts pushing the cart like it's a sports car and you're in the passenger seat, it's time for a reality check. Love is all about teamwork, and in the grocery store, that means equally sharing the burden of the cart's weight, not turning it into a bumper car experience. If you can survive the cart chaos together, you just might be able to face anything life throws your way.

Next up: the produce section. Here, love is tested in the form of fruit selection. You pick up a perfectly ripe avocado, only to have your partner declare that it's "too squishy." This is where negotiations begin. Do you abandon your quest for the perfect guacamole, or do you stand your ground like a knight defending a castle? The produce section can quickly become a battlefield of opinions, but if you can reach a compromise between the "squishy avocado" and "the rock-hard one," you're destined for culinary greatness. After all, who doesn't love a good guacamole debate?

As you make your way to the checkout line, the final love test looms: the impulse buys. Will you be able to resist the siren call of the chocolate bars or the latest trendy snack? This is where trust and shared values come into play. If your partner throws a six-pack of soda into the cart while you're trying to stick to a healthy diet, a silent war can erupt. But if you both can laugh off the temptation and agree that maybe the overpriced artisanal chips can wait until next week, your bond will only strengthen. After all, love is about making choices together, and sometimes those choices include saying no to overpriced snacks.

Finally, as you leave the store with your loot, take a moment to appreciate the absurdity of it all. Grocery shopping isn't just about buying food; it's about navigating the relationship minefield, complete with cart collisions and heated debates over snack selections. It's about finding joy in the little things, like the shared laughter when you both realize you forgot the milk again. So, the next time you gear up for a grocery run, remember that it's not just a shopping trip; it's a love expedition. And if you can survive it together, there's no doubt that your love is as nourishing as the meals you'll prepare.

Netflix Decisions: Choosing a Show Without a Fight

Netflix, the modern-day oracle of entertainment, offers us an endless scroll of options that can feel more overwhelming than choosing a partner. You and your significant other settle down for a cozy night in, armed with popcorn and a blanket, only to find yourselves engaged in an epic showdown over what to watch. The battle lines are drawn: one wants a heartwarming rom-com, while the other is set on a gritty documentary about the history of shoelaces. Ah, the joys of love and Netflix!

First, let's talk about the infamous "I don't care, you choose" line. This phrase is a classic trap, akin to saying, "I love all your friends equally." It sounds great on the surface, but deep down, it's a ticking time bomb. The moment you pick a show that doesn't meet the unspoken criteria of your partner's secret wishlist, you're suddenly the villain of the evening. You'll hear a dramatic sigh that could rival any Shakespearean monologue. The trick is to pretend you care about the latest true-crime series while secretly hoping for a light-hearted adventure.

Next comes the dreaded scrolling phase, where you both swipe through titles as if you're trying to find the perfect avocado at the grocery store. "How about this one?" you ask, only to be met with a dubious eyebrow raise. You quickly realize that selecting a show is less about the actual content and more about navigating the mine-field of your partner's preferences. Remember, it's not just about finding something to watch; it's about keeping the peace. So, brace yourself for the ultimate compromise: something that's half romantic, half thrilling, and definitely has at least one talking animal.

If you're still not on the same page after all this, it may be time to employ the classic "rock-paper-scissors" technique. It's simple, fair, and a little ridiculous—much like love itself. You could argue that it's a time-honored method of decision-making that has survived the test of time, much like your relationship. However, be wary; if one of you is a sore loser, this could devolve into a full-blown debate about the unfairness of life, love, and the algorithmic injustice of Netflix.

Finally, once you've reached a consensus—perhaps after a few rounds of negotiation and maybe even a snack break—there's that moment of joy when you finally press play. You snuggle in, ready to enjoy your selected masterpiece, only to find out that it's the same show you watched last week. But hey, at least you're together, right? In the grand scheme of love, it's those little moments of compromise and laughter that count. And who knows? Maybe the next time you sit down for a Netflix decision, you'll both just agree to watch whatever is trending, and save the bickering for the next dinner party.

Weekend Chores: Love is in the Dust Bunnies

When it comes to love, we often envision candlelit dinners and romantic getaways, but let's be real: most of us spend the majority of our weekends elbow-deep in the less glamorous side of life—chores. Yes, the very act of scrubbing toilets and vacuuming dust bunnies can be a surprisingly effective love language. After all, nothing says "I love you" quite like removing the evidence of last week's popcorn binge from the couch cushions.

Picture this: it's Saturday morning, and the sun is shining. You and your partner have the whole day ahead of you. Instead of diving into a Netflix marathon, you decide to tackle the mountain of laundry that's been threatening to avalanche onto the floor. As you sort colors from whites, you can't help but chuckle at how your relationship has evolved. Remember when you used to spend weekends dreaming about your future? Now, you're dreaming about the day you'll find the bottom of the laundry basket.

As you fold those shirts, you start to reminisce about the first time you saw each other in a laundry room, both awkwardly trying to impress the other with your choice of fabric softener. Who knew that detergent could be such a turn-on? Fast forward to now, and you're both arguing about the merits of hot versus cold washes. The laundry may feel like a mundane chore, but it's also a bonding experience. Each argument and shared laugh over sock mismatches is a thread weaving you closer together, even if it occasionally unravels into a sock war.

Then there's the ever-popular chore of vacuuming, where the real magic happens. Is there anything more romantic than watching your partner skillfully maneuver the vacuum cleaner, dodging furniture like a ninja while simultaneously trying to avoid getting stuck on the carpet? You can't help but giggle as they attempt to assert their dominance over the dust bunnies that have clearly formed a small army in the corner. This is a real-life battle of love against grime, and you're both on the frontline, armed with a vacuum and a sense of humor.

By the end of your weekend chore marathon, you may be covered in dust, but you're also covered in love—sticky and slightly disheveled but undeniably closer than when you started. The magic lies not just in the completion of each task, but in the shared laughter, the playful banter, and the teamwork. So, the next time you're contemplating how to spend your weekend, remember: love is indeed in the dust bunnies, and sometimes the most romantic moments are found in the least expected places, like the laundry room or the vacuum closet.

Love in the Digital Age

Dating Apps: Swiping Right on Life

In the digital age, dating apps have transformed the romantic landscape into a virtual buffet of potential partners. Picture yourself at a buffet: there's a little something for everyone, but you also need to navigate the occasional mystery meat. Swiping right has become an art form, with users deftly flicking their fingers across screens, judging suitability based on a few curated images and a catchy tagline. Who knew that a well-placed avocado toast photo could be the key to someone's heart? However, let's not forget that behind every profile lies a person, and sometimes that person is just as confusing as a riddle wrapped in an enigma.

The beauty of dating apps lies in their ability to connect people from all walks of life, but the process can feel like a game show where you're both contestant and host. How many times have you sat there, swiping through profiles, wondering if you should pick the one with the dog, the one with the mysterious quote about adventure, or the one who just seems to have a perpetual vacation tan? It's like trying to choose the best flavor of ice cream when you know you're lactose intolerant. The pressure is real, and let's be honest, sometimes you just want to swipe right on the entire lineup and hope for the best.

Of course, with great power comes great responsibility. The responsibility of crafting the perfect profile that balances charm and intrigue without sounding like a human ad for a used car. "I enjoy long walks on the beach" is a classic, but let's be real: who wants to walk when you can just lounge with a drink in hand? Navigating conversations can be even trickier, as you try to decipher whether the other person is a genuine match or just a master of small talk with a penchant for emojis. Remember, it's not about how many times you can use "LOL" in one conversation; it's about finding someone who can make you chuckle in real life.

As you dive deeper into this pixelated romance, prepare yourself for the inevitable "ghosting" phenomenon. One moment, you're sharing existential musings about the meaning of life, and the next, you're left wondering if they've been abducted by aliens. Ghosting is the dating app equivalent of being left on read, and it's more common than finding a decent avocado at the grocery store. It's enough to make anyone question whether love is truly what it is or just a series of unfortunate events played out on a smartphone screen.

Despite the quirks and challenges, dating apps offer the possibility of finding a connection that transcends the virtual world. They provide a platform for meeting individuals you might never cross paths with otherwise—like that one guy who collects vintage typewriters or the woman who has a passion for competitive cheese rolling. Love, in all its unpredictable forms, often arrives when you least expect it. So, as you swipe right on life, remember to keep an open mind, a sense of humor, and perhaps a backup plan for when things get a little too cheesy.

Social Media: Sharing Love or Oversharing?

Social media has transformed the way we express love, turning romantic gestures into public spectacles. Gone are the days of sweet handwritten notes and intimate dinners; now, love is just a hashtag away. You can declare your affection with a perfectly filtered photo captioned "My forever" or a video of your partner trying to cook dinner (which is really just an elaborate way to say, "Look how cute they are when they set the kitchen on fire"). But with this newfound public display of affection comes the question: are we sharing love, or are we just oversharing?

Let's take a moment to consider the fine line between sharing love and oversharing. There's a sweet spot where your love story can inspire others—a cute couple dancing in their living room, a lovely anniversary post, or even a heartfelt message about how your partner makes you better. But then there's the other side, where things get a bit cringeworthy. You know, the couple that posts daily updates on their breakfast choices together or the ones who feel the need to document every single fight and makeup session. I mean, who really wants to know about the time you had an argument over who left the toilet seat up? Spoiler alert: nobody!

Let's not forget those couples who have taken it to the extreme with relationship goals. You know those perfectly curated feeds that look like they just stepped out of a romance movie? The couple frolicking on a beach at sunset, followed by a post about how they "just can't live without each other." Meanwhile, in reality, one of them is probably hiding behind the camera, rolling their eyes at the whole charade. The truth is, love isn't always picture-perfect; sometimes it's messy, chaotic, and full of inside jokes that no one else would understand. So why not embrace the glorious messiness of love instead of trying to fit it into a social media box?

And let's not overlook the unsolicited advice that comes with sharing love online. Post a picture of you and your partner on a hike, and suddenly you're bombarded with comments like, "You should get married!" or "When are the babies coming?" It's as if people forget that love is about the journey, not the destination. Maybe the couple just wanted to enjoy a peaceful walk without a side of pressure! It's a fine balance between sharing joy and inviting the world to weigh in on your relationship decisions. Sometimes, it feels less like a celebration of love and more like a social media version of "The Hunger Games"—may the odds be ever in your favor!

In the end, social media can be a wonderful tool for sharing love, but it's essential to navigate it with a sense of humor and a healthy dose of self-awareness. While it's tempting to showcase every sweet moment, remember that love thrives in the genuine and the imperfect. So, go ahead and post that adorable picture of you both, but maybe leave out the details of your latest spat over laundry. After all, love is meant to be shared, but not in a way that turns your relationship into a reality show. Embrace the joy, the laughter, and even the chaos—because love, in all its forms, is what it is.

Virtual Love: When Your Heart is Just a Click Away

In the age of technology, love has taken on a whole new form, and it's often just a click away. Virtual love is like that mysterious box of chocolates you get on Valentine's Day—sometimes you bite into a delightful caramel, and other times, you're left chewing on something that resembles a rubber band. Online dating apps have turned the pursuit of romance into a digital scavenger hunt where the only thing you can find with certainty is a plethora of blurry selfies and a few unsolicited cat pictures. Ah, modern love!

Navigating the world of virtual relationships is akin to walking through a minefield while blindfolded and wearing roller skates. You swipe right, and suddenly you're in a whirlwind of emojis, memes, and awkward small talk about the weather. Why is it that every single person seems to love hiking, even if they've never stepped outside their apartment? It's as though the great outdoors has become a virtual myth, like Bigfoot or that one friend who actually enjoys doing their taxes. But here's the kicker: all that digital chatting can lead to some surprisingly deep connections— assuming you don't accidentally send a heart emoji to your boss.

Then comes the moment you decide to take the plunge and meet in person. The thrill of anticipation is only matched by the sheer terror of realizing you might have misrepresented yourself just a tad. Did you really mention that you once ran a marathon when you actually just ran to the fridge during a Netflix binge? The pressure is on, and suddenly your online persona must transform into a real-life human being. Spoiler alert: it's not always a seamless transition. You may find that your date shows up looking like a supermodel while you resemble a raccoon that just emerged from an all-night pizza party.

Of course, virtual love is not without its benefits. You can date while wearing sweatpants, and nobody is the wiser. There's something incredibly liberating about being able to enjoy a romantic dinner over a video call, with the only thing on your mind being whether you can successfully hide your messy living room from the camera. And let's not forget about those heartwarming late-night conversations that can range from philosophical debates about the meaning of life to arguments over the best pizza toppings. Who knew love could come with such a side of pineapple?

As we navigate this quirky landscape of virtual love, it's essential to remember that despite the digital barriers, the core of human connection remains the same. Whether your heart is ensconced in a pixelated format or bursting forth in real-life encounters, love is still love—complete with its own sweet and sour moments. So, embrace the adventure, laugh at the mishaps, and keep your heart open. After all, you never know when the next click might lead you to a love story worth telling—complete with all the awkward pauses and delightful surprises that come with it.

Lessons Learned the Hard Way

The Ex Files: What Not to Do Again

In the wild world of romance, the Ex Files serve as a warning beacon for those brave enough to navigate the treacherous waters of love. Picture this: you're cruising along on the love boat, and suddenly, there's an iceberg labeled "Ex." It's not just any iceberg; it's the one that sunk the Titanic. So, let's dive into the hilariously cringe-worthy lessons learned from past relationships that should come with a "do not repeat" sign.

First up, we have the classic blunder of the "Texting Ex." You know, the one where you're feeling all warm and fuzzy after a few too many glasses of wine and decide it's a brilliant idea to send a heartfelt message to your former flame. Spoiler alert: It's never a good idea. If your ex is on your mind post-wine, it's probably a sign that you should be hitting the gym instead of the "send" button. Trust me, the only thing you'll achieve is a new level of embarrassment and a new reason to block them on social media.

Next on our list is the "Over-Analysis Olympics." This is where you dissect every word, emoji, and punctuation mark from your last conversation like it's a Shakespearean sonnet. You might think you're Sherlock Holmes on the case of "What Did They Mean?" but in reality, you're more like a raccoon rummaging through trash. Instead of gaining clarity, you gain a headache and a new appreciation for ice cream. Remember, if you find yourself crafting a flowchart to decipher your ex's behavior, it's time to put the magnifying glass down and step away from the drama.

Let's not forget about the "Social Media Stalker" phase. You know, the one where you've turned into a detective, scrolling through every photo and post your ex has made since your breakup like it's the latest season of your favorite show. You're not just a casual observer; you're an undercover agent with a mission. The results? A cocktail of jealousy, confusion, and the realization that maybe you should have just invested that time in learning a new hobby. Spoiler: your ex is not going to change their mind because you liked their 5-month-old vacation photo.

Now, we arrive at the "Rebound Regret." This is the moment you think dating someone new will magically erase your ex from your mind. But here's the catch: if you're still hung up on your previous relationship, your new partner is likely to feel like a placeholder, and that's not fair to anyone involved. You're not a vending machine where you can just swap out one snack for another. Take the time to heal, and don't drag someone else into your emotional baggage claim. Trust me, nobody wants to be the emotional equivalent of a third wheel.

In the end, every misstep in the Ex Files is an opportunity to learn and laugh at our past selves. Love is a journey full of bumps, bruises, and plenty of awkward moments. The key is to take those experiences, wrap them up in a humorous bow, and move forward with the wisdom that comes from knowing exactly what not to do again. So, let's raise a glass to our past loves—may they forever remain in the archives of "What Not to Do Again."

The "We Need to Talk" Moment: A Comedy of Timing

There's a universal truth in relationships: the "We Need to Talk" moment is like a surprise party you never wanted but can't escape. You know that feeling when your partner suddenly shifts from casual banter to a serious tone, and your stomach drops faster than a roller coaster? It's as if they've just revealed that the last slice of pizza has been thrown away. The timing is always impeccable—right after you've binge-watched a series on love and romance, only to find yourself knee-deep in a conversation that feels more like a trip to the dentist than a heart-to-heart.

Picture this: you're snuggled up on the couch, popcorn in hand, and your partner looks at you with those big, innocent eyes. You think they're about to confess their undying love, but instead, you get, "We need to talk." Suddenly, the romantic music in your head turns into a suspenseful thriller score. You go from dreaming of sunsets on a beach to imagining a courtroom drama where you're the defendant. Who knew love could feel like a legal proceeding? The stakes are high, and your mind races through a checklist of possible crimes against love you might have committed, including eating their leftover fries or forgetting their birthday.

Timing, of course, is everything. The classic "We Need to Talk" moment usually strikes when you least expect it—like when you're still half-asleep and trying to figure out if the person in front of you is your partner or a very confused burglar. Why do these conversations never happen after a romantic dinner? They seem to lurk in the shadows, waiting for the precise moment when you've just let your guard down. It's as if the universe has a twisted sense of humor, orchestrating these scenarios for maximum comedic effect. You can almost hear the laugh track playing in the background as you scramble to keep the conversation from spiraling into chaos.

Then comes the dreaded question: "What's wrong?" You try to recall if you left the toilet seat up or if you've been hogging the remote control. But the reality is, the "What's wrong?" moment often leads to a rabbit hole of misunderstandings. One minute you're talking about your Netflix queue, and the next, you're debating whether leaving the dishes in the sink constitutes a declaration of war. It's as if love has a hidden manual that no one gives you, filled with rules that change daily and are often open to interpretation. The beauty of it all, however, is that these moments, while fraught with tension, often lead to the funniest stories later on, once everyone has calmed down and had a good laugh.

In the end, the "We Need to Talk" moment serves as a reminder that love isn't just about the rosy sunsets and candlelit dinners. It's about navigating the awkward, the absurd, and the downright hilarious aspects of sharing your life with another human being. So the next time you find yourself in one of those cringe-worthy conversations, take a deep breath and try to find the humor in it. After all, love is what it is—a wild ride filled with unexpected twists, and sometimes, you just have to laugh your way through the confusion.

Moving On: How to Laugh at Your Past

Moving on from our past can feel like trying to fit into last year's jeans: it's uncomfortable, awkward, and sometimes downright impossible. We've all been there, right? You're scrolling through old photos, and suddenly you're confronted with a picture of yourself in a questionable hairstyle or a fashion choice that should have been left in the depths of the closet. The key to moving on is learning to laugh at these moments. Yes, those embarrassing memories can become the punchlines of your life's stand-up routine. Instead of cringing, embrace the absurdity of your past choices; after all, they make for great stories at parties!

Let's be real: we've all had that phase where we thought we were the next great romantic hero, only to discover we were actually more of a romantic zero. Remember that time you tried to win over your crush with a grand gesture, like serenading them in public? Spoiler alert: it usually doesn't end well. The ability to look back on these moments with humor is liberating. It's like a mental detox for your heart. You're not just shedding the weight of past relationships; you're also shedding the embarrassment of those cringe-worthy attempts at love. So, go ahead and chuckle at your younger self. They were trying their best, but they probably also believed that wearing socks with sandals was a bold fashion statement.

As you sift through the memories, you'll notice a pattern: the recurring bad dates, the awkward conversations, and the moments that make you question your judgment. Instead of wallowing in self-pity, turn those experiences into comedy gold. Share them with friends over drinks. Nothing bonds people quite like laughter over shared relationships failures. Plus, you might find that others are eager to share their own hilariously disastrous tales. This collective chuckling not only helps you heal but also reminds you that you're not alone. Everyone has a past filled with questionable decisions and a few regrettable haircuts.

The art of moving on is also about recognizing that your past doesn't define you. Sure, you might have made some cringeworthy choices, but those moments are merely chapters in your love story. They add richness and flavor, like the weird ingredient in your favorite dish that you can't quite place but makes it extraordinary. So, every time you feel tempted to dwell on what went wrong, remind yourself that these experiences are what make you relatable. They're the seasoning that adds depth to your character. Plus, let's face it, who doesn't love a good underdog story?

Ultimately, learning to laugh at your past is a powerful tool in your journey toward love. It allows you to approach new relationships with a light heart and an open mind. When you're not weighed down by the baggage of yesterday, you create space for the possibilities of tomorrow. So, the next time you find yourself reminiscing about that awkward first date or the time you accidentally texted your ex instead of your best friend, chuckle, take a deep breath, and remember: love is a wild ride, and sometimes, the best way to enjoy the journey is to laugh at the bumps along the way.

The Joy of Lasting Love

The Comfort of Routine: When Boring is Beautiful

In a world that constantly bombards us with excitement and novelty, it's easy to overlook the charm of routine. Picture this: you wake up, brew your coffee, and settle into your favorite chair. The sun filters through the window, and the smell of toast wafts through the air. It might sound like a scene from a sitcom, but these seemingly mundane moments are where the magic happens. Routine is like that dependable friend who always shows up with snacks at the party—unassuming yet essential. Who needs roller coasters when you can ride the wave of a perfectly timed 7:00 AM coffee?

Now, let's address the elephant in the room: the word "boring." It's a term that often gets a bad rap, as if it's the villain in a romantic comedy. But consider this: boring is the unsung hero of love. It's the predictable rhythm that allows us to dance together without stepping on each other's toes. In relationships, the beauty of routine is akin to that favorite song you could play on repeat without getting tired of it. Those Saturday mornings spent in pajamas, arguing over the best way to make scrambled eggs, might not make headlines, but they certainly build a solid foundation for love to flourish.

Embracing routine means saying yes to the little things that add up to a whole lot of love. Think of it as the equivalent of wearing your most comfortable sweatpants on a Friday night instead of squeezing into those unforgiving jeans. There's nothing glamorous about eating takeout while binge-watching your favorite show, yet it's in those moments that you often find the deepest connections. Who knew that arguing over which movie to watch or fighting for the last piece of pizza could be the glue that holds your relationship together? It's practically a comedy sketch waiting to happen!

Of course, there will always be moments when spontaneity seems more appealing. Who doesn't want to be swept off their feet by a surprise trip to Paris? But let's face it: the chances of getting caught in traffic or battling a language barrier often overshadow the romance of the unexpected. Routine offers a comforting predictability that allows love to thrive without the anxiety of planning the next big adventure. After all, nothing says "I love you" quite like knowing what your partner's favorite pizza topping is and being ready with an extra slice.

In the grand scheme of love, the beauty of routine lies in its ability to create a safe space for vulnerability and growth. It's the blanket fort of relationships, where you can laugh, cry, and share your dreams without fear of judgment. So, the next time you find yourself in a "boring" moment, take a step back and appreciate the beauty in its simplicity. Love may not always be a whirlwind of excitement, but it certainly can be a cozy, delightful routine that warms your heart—preferably while you're both still in your pajamas.

Growing Together: Love After the Honeymoon Phase

Ah, the honeymoon phase—those blissful days when love feels like a never-ending rom-com, complete with cheesy one-liners and spontaneous dance parties in the living room. You know, the time when you could stare into each other's eyes over dinner and talk about your favorite ice cream flavors for hours without a hint of boredom. But as the dust settles and reality sets in, that sparkly sheen can dull a bit, like the aftermath of a wild party where someone forgot to take out the trash. So, how do we transition from the fairytale to the everyday without losing our minds or each other?

First things first: embrace the quirks. You know what I'm talking about—those little idiosyncrasies that seemed endearing when you were head over heels but now seem slightly maddening. Perhaps your partner has a unique method of folding laundry that resembles origami gone wrong, or maybe they insist on putting ketchup on everything. Instead of rolling your eyes and plotting their demise, find the humor in it. Celebrate that oddball personality; let's face it, if life were a sitcom, these moments would be the punchlines. Laughter becomes the glue that helps you navigate the mundane while keeping the love alive.

Next, it's time to redefine your romantic pursuits. Gone are the days of surprise candlelit dinners and spontaneous weekend getaways (at least, for now). But that doesn't mean romance is dead; it just means it's taken on a new form. Picture this: a Friday night Netflix binge with homemade popcorn, or a cooking disaster where you both end up covered in flour but giggling like kids. These simple moments can be just as fulfilling as those grand gestures, and let's be real, who doesn't love a little chaos in the kitchen? It's a bonding experience like no other—plus, you always have the option of ordering pizza when things go awry.

Communication remains your best friend, and no, we're not talking about the "let's sit down and have a serious conversation" kind. Instead, think of it as creating your own secret language. Develop inside jokes that only the two of you understand. This can be anything from silly nicknames to ridiculous hand signals that save you from a full-blown argument in public. The goal is to keep the lines of communication open while adding a dose of playfulness. Who knew that discussing the grocery list could turn into a hilarious debate over whether avocados should be classified as a fruit or a vegetable?

Finally, remember that growing together means accepting change. As time goes on, you might find yourselves evolving in unexpected ways. Maybe you've developed a newfound passion for pottery, and your partner prefers to binge-watch documentaries on the history of cheese (yes, that's a thing). Instead of viewing these differences as a rift, consider them as opportunities for growth. Encourage each other to explore these interests, and who knows, you might just end up with a unique pottery piece that doubles as a cheese platter. It's all about finding that sweet balance between individuality and togetherness, which can be as delicious as a perfectly paired wine and cheese.

In the end, love after the honeymoon phase doesn't have to be a scary descent into the abyss of boredom. By embracing quirks, redefining romance, fostering playful communication, and accepting change, you can create a relationship that's not only fun but also deeply fulfilling. So, grab your partner, share a laugh, and remember: love is what it is, and it's often a lot more entertaining than any movie could portray.

Celebrating Love: The Little Things that Matter Most

In the grand scheme of love, it's the little things that often steal the spotlight and make our hearts do a little jig. You know, those moments that don't require a grand gesture or a five-star restaurant reservation. Like when your partner brings you a cup of coffee just the way you like it—hot, strong, and with just enough cream to make the barista jealous. You might find yourself thinking, "Is this love, or is it just really good coffee?" Spoiler alert: it's both! It's those caffeine-fueled acts of kindness that remind us love can be as simple as a well-timed caffeine fix.

Let's not forget the magic found in shared inside jokes. You know you've hit the love jackpot when you and your partner can communicate in a series of quirky looks and nonsensical phrases that make absolutely no sense to anyone else. Whether it's a silly nickname or a hilarious mishap from last summer's camping trip, these little snippets of shared humor create a bond that feels unbreakable. It's like having a secret language that only you two speak, which is equal parts adorable and slightly absurd. And honestly, who wouldn't want to explain to their friends why they can't stop laughing over "the great spaghetti incident of 2020"?

Then there are the spontaneous dance parties in the living room, which are the unsung heroes of love celebrations. Picture this: you're folding laundry, and suddenly your favorite song comes on. Instead of just nodding your head in rhythm while sorting socks, your partner grabs your hand, and within seconds, you're spinning around the room like you're auditioning for a musical. Sure, you might trip over the dog or knock a lamp over, but what's love without a little chaos? Those moments remind us that love doesn't have to be serious; it can be silly, spontaneous, and full of laughter.

Speaking of laughter, there's nothing quite like the joy of sharing food. Whether it's splitting a ridiculously oversized slice of pizza or engaging in a heated debate over the last piece of chocolate cake, food has a magical way of bringing people together. It's in those moments of culinary chaos where love thrives. You might find yourselves fighting over the breadsticks or making a mess trying to cook a new recipe. But at the end of the day, it's not about the food but the memories created—like the time you almost set the kitchen on fire trying to impress your partner with your "culinary skills."

Finally, let's talk about those mundane moments that somehow become extraordinary. When you sit together on the couch, watching your favorite show for the fifth time, or when you're both too lazy to move and decide that pizza delivery is the best plan of action. These seemingly insignificant instances are where love truly flourishes. They remind us that love is not just about grand declarations or candlelit dinners but also about finding comfort in the ordinary. So, celebrate those little things, because in the end, it's the quirks, the laughter, and those perfectly imperfect moments that make love what it is—wonderful, messy, and oh-so-precious.

About the Author

George Hatcher is a man who has always believed that the world is full of opportunities waiting for those bold enough to seize them. With a ninth-grade education and a wealth of unique experiences, he has faced the ups and downs of life head-on. At the age of 20, while serving time, George took the initiative to complete the assignments and tests necessary to earn his high school diploma. His own life is a treasure trove of stories waiting to be uncovered.

Over the years, George has enjoyed a diverse career as an entrepreneur, consultant, and strategist. He has served as a peacemaker for athletes and their parents, as well as a crisis management advisor for physicians and attorneys, achieving considerable success in client development and public relations. He is a licensed boxing manager in California, though he currently has no boxers signed.

George has logged over 200,000 air miles annually through business travel and pleasure trips with his wife. However, since the onset of COVID-19 in 2020, his travel has come to a halt. Now, in retirement, George finds that life remains an ongoing adventure. Unfortunately, he is fighting several new battles that he never anticipated, yet he continues to discover something new with each step.

As a passionate storyteller, George has published a dozen books and finds immense joy in writing. With the world opening up again, he has seized the opportunity to immerse himself fully in his literary pursuits. He currently resides in Rancho Mirage, California, with his wife, Molly, his partner for 59 years, and their home is filled with three cats and two macaws. Each experience in his life has taught him invaluable lessons about adaptability, perseverance, and a touch of luck. Like the person who hits their head just to feel the pleasure of stopping, George has made his share of mistakes—some more than once. He hopes others can learn from them as he has.

Now devoted entirely to writing, George Hatcher invites others to join him on this remarkable journey, filled with lessons and stories that showcase the beauty of life's unpredictability.

A longer bio is on his website at
http://georgehatcher.com/bio/bio.html

www.ingramcontent.com/pod-product-compliance
Lightning Source LLC
Chambersburg PA
CBHW070943120726
47908CB00005BA/1501